The Fox on the Box

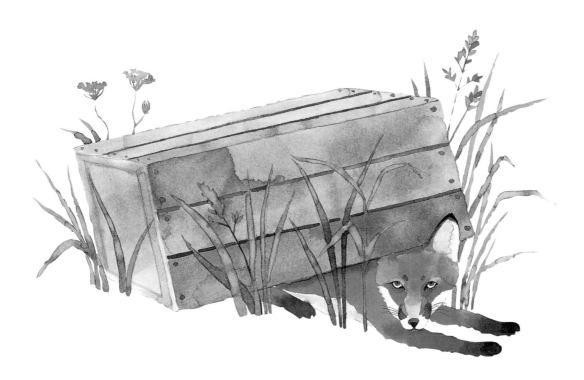

Written by
Barbara Gregorich

Illustrated by
Robert Masheris

The fox sat on the box.

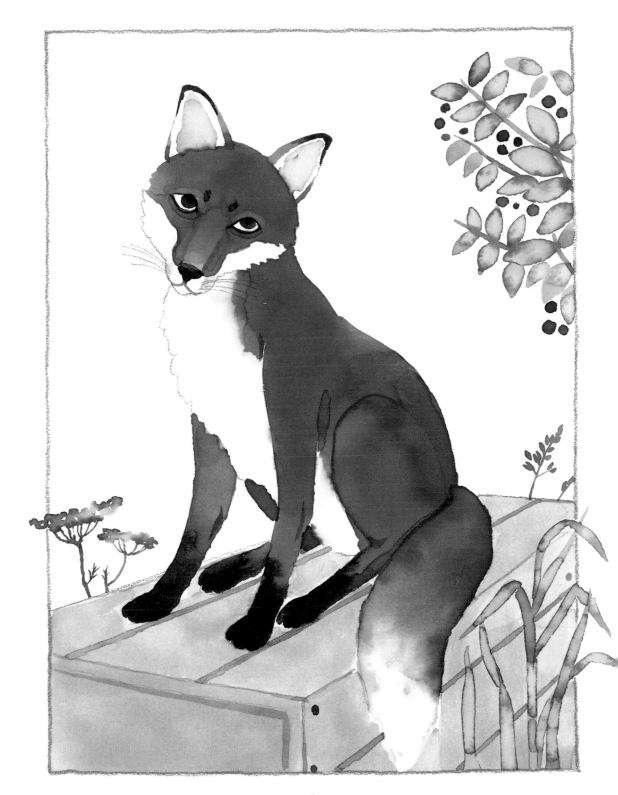

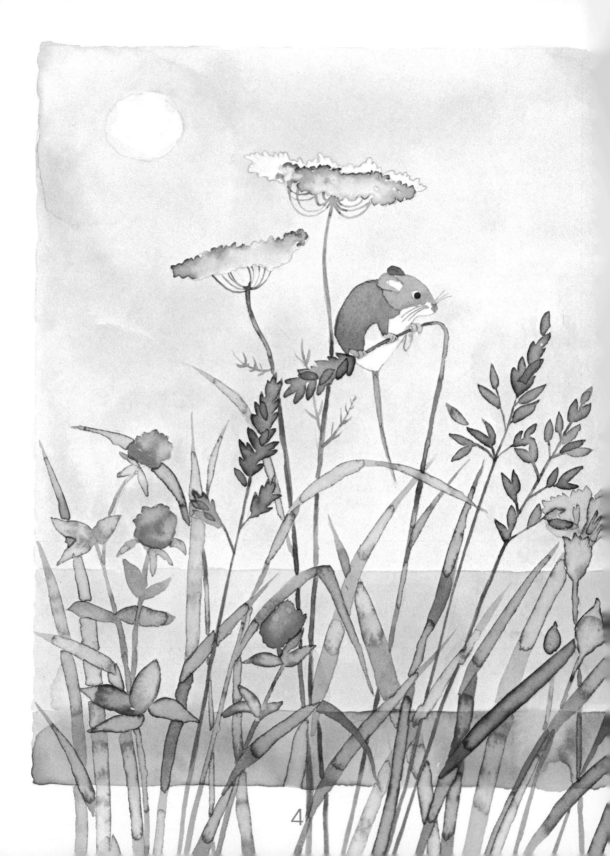

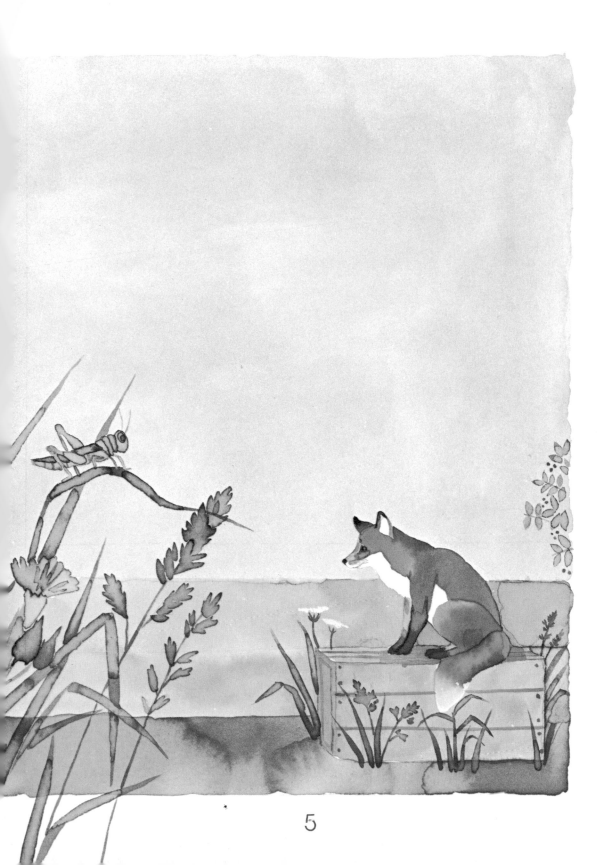

The fox ate on the box.

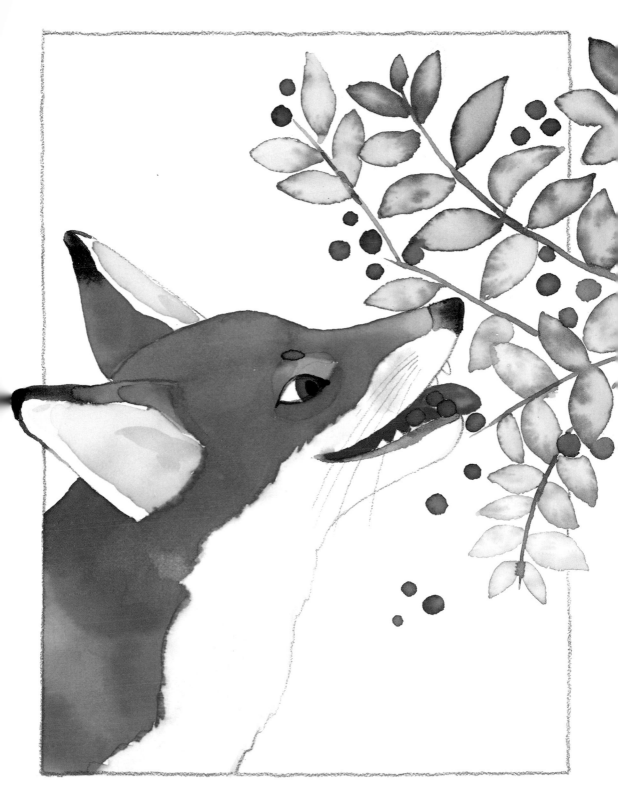

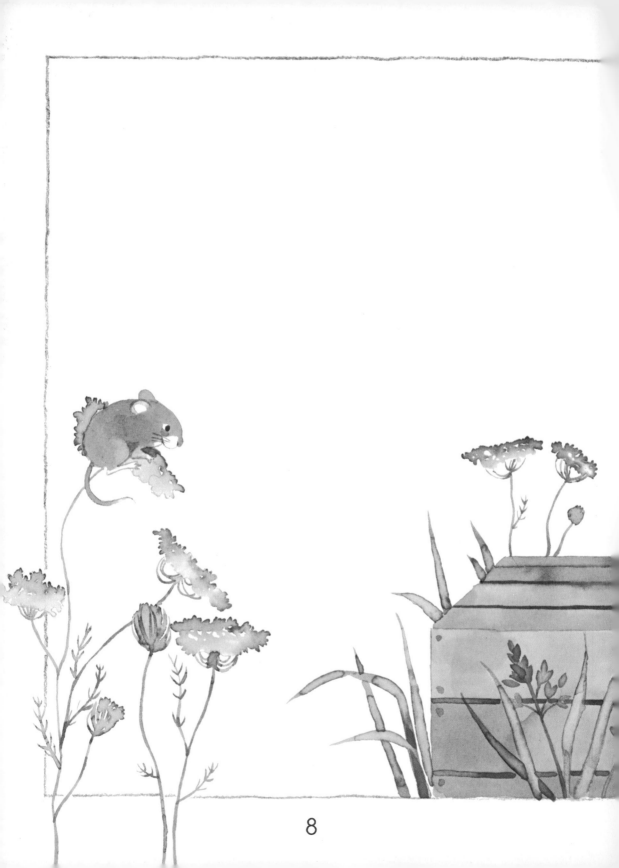

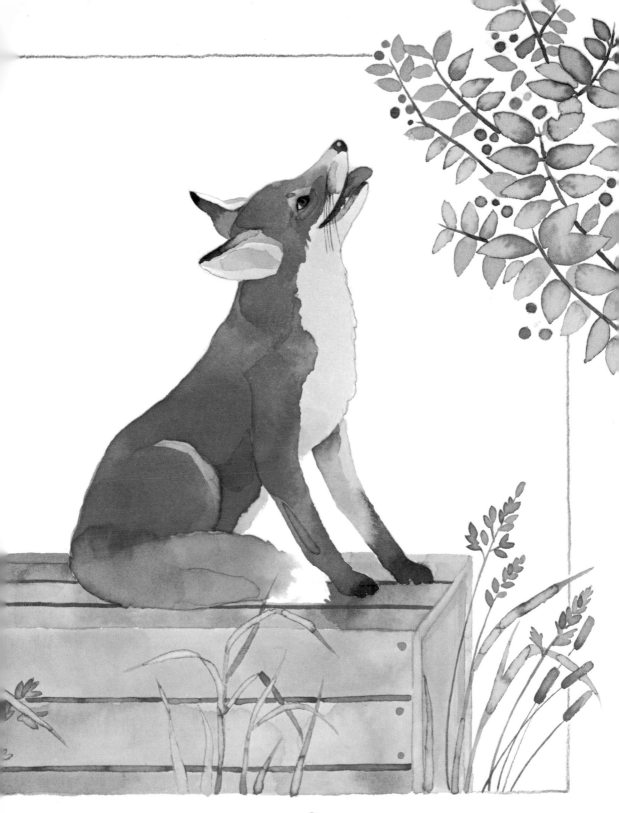

The fox played on the box.

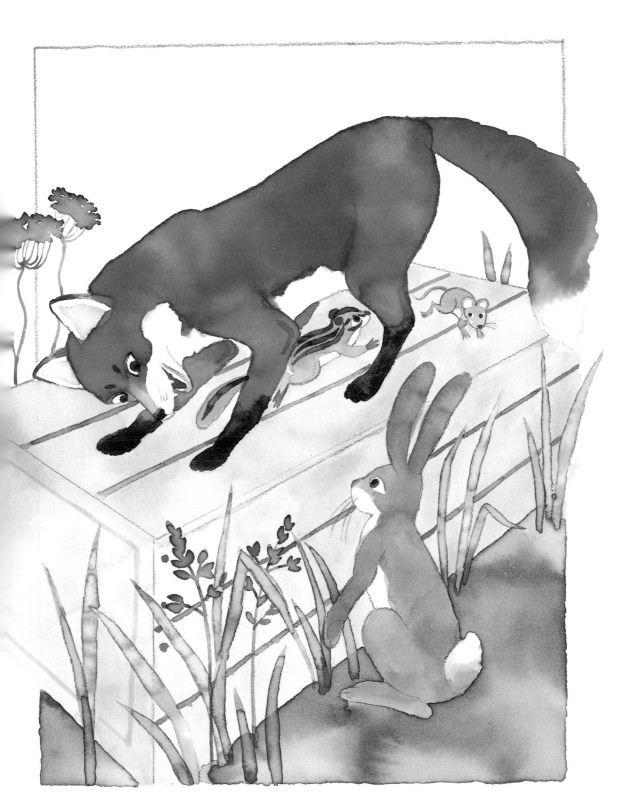

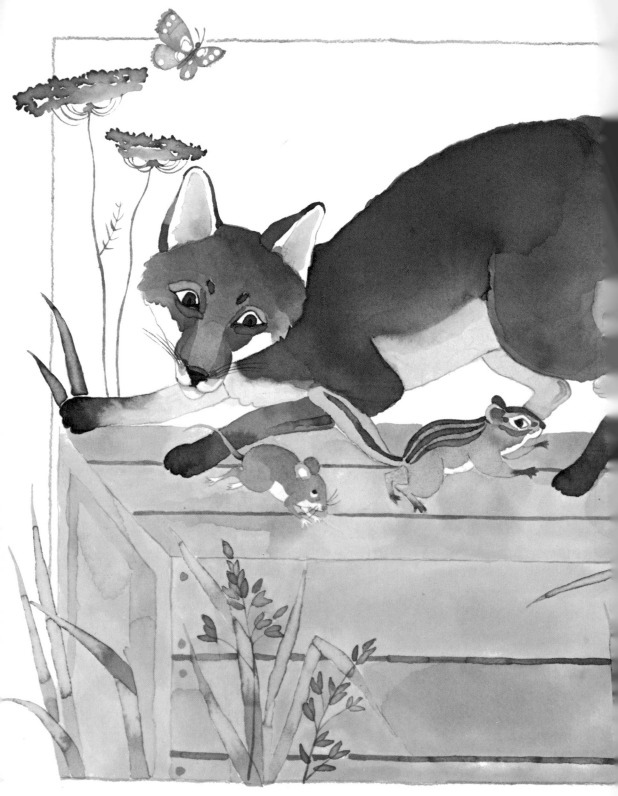

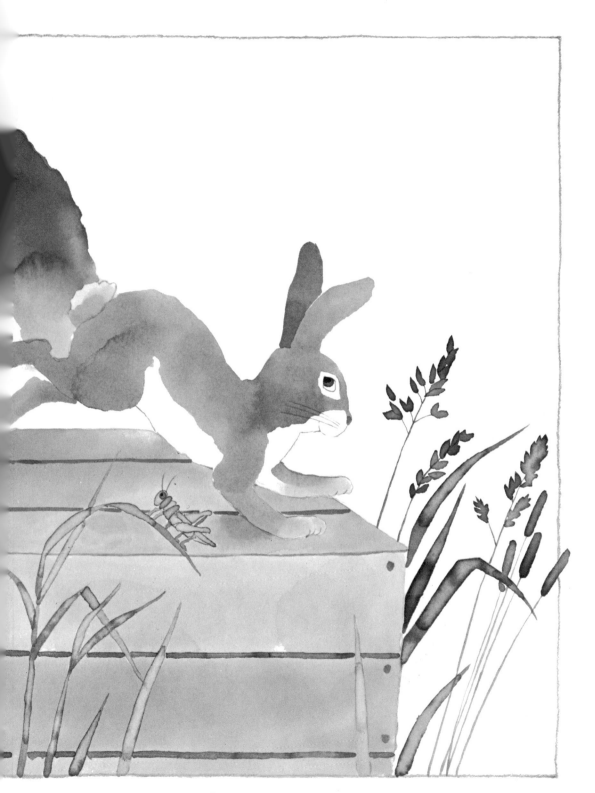

The fox jumped over the box.

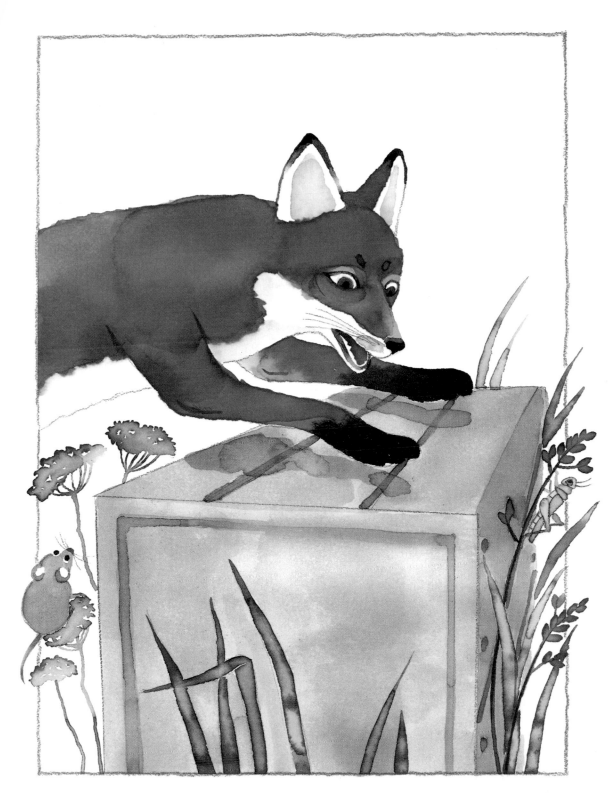

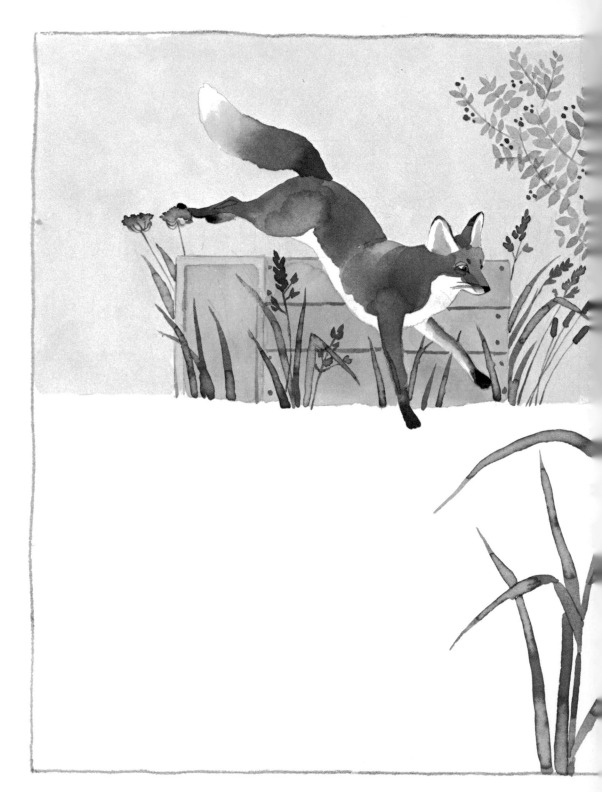

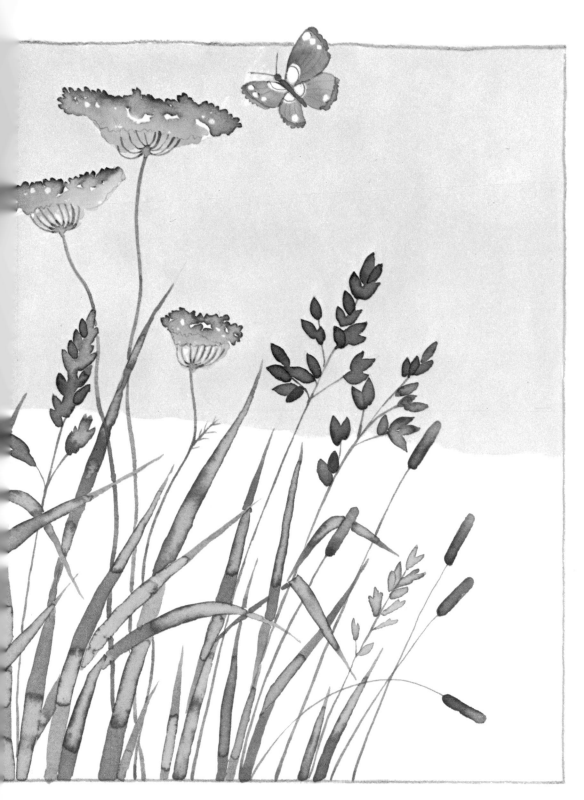

The fox jumped on the box.

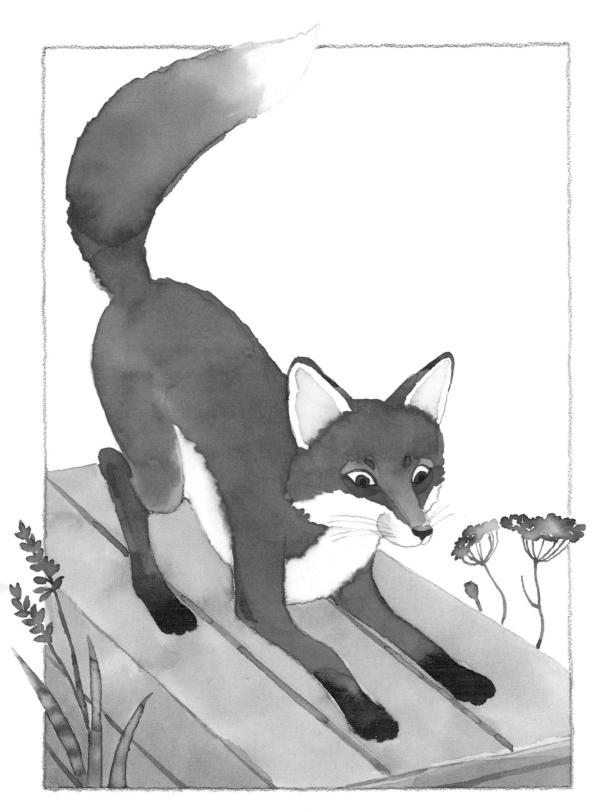

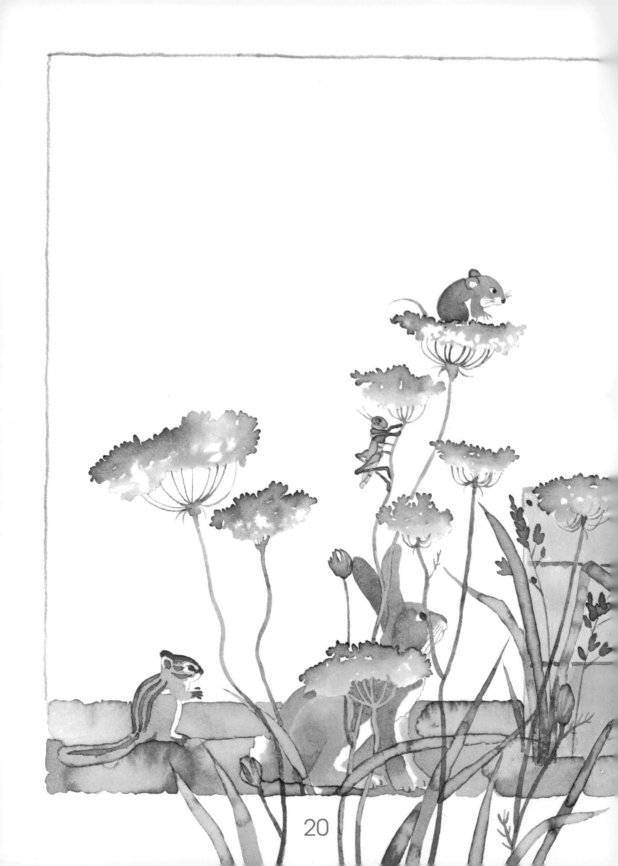

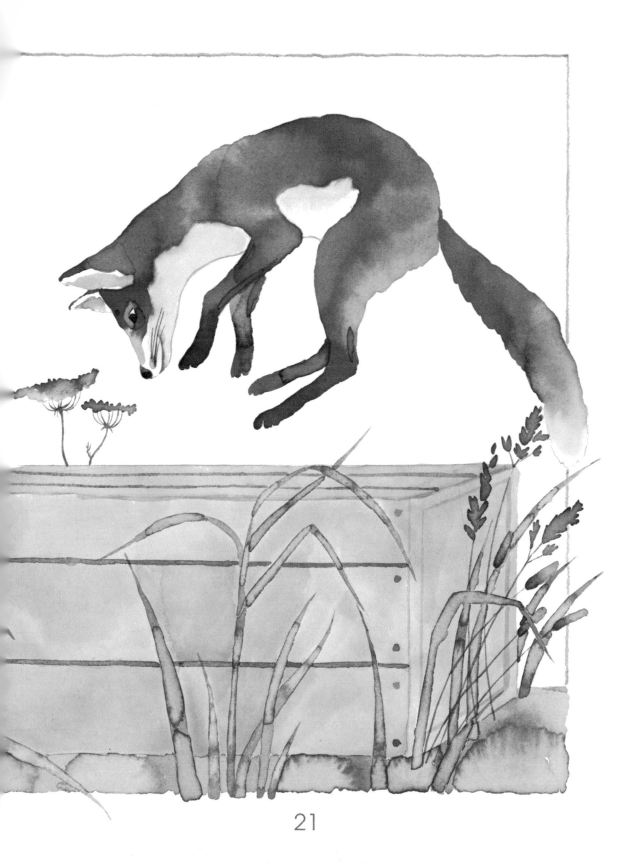

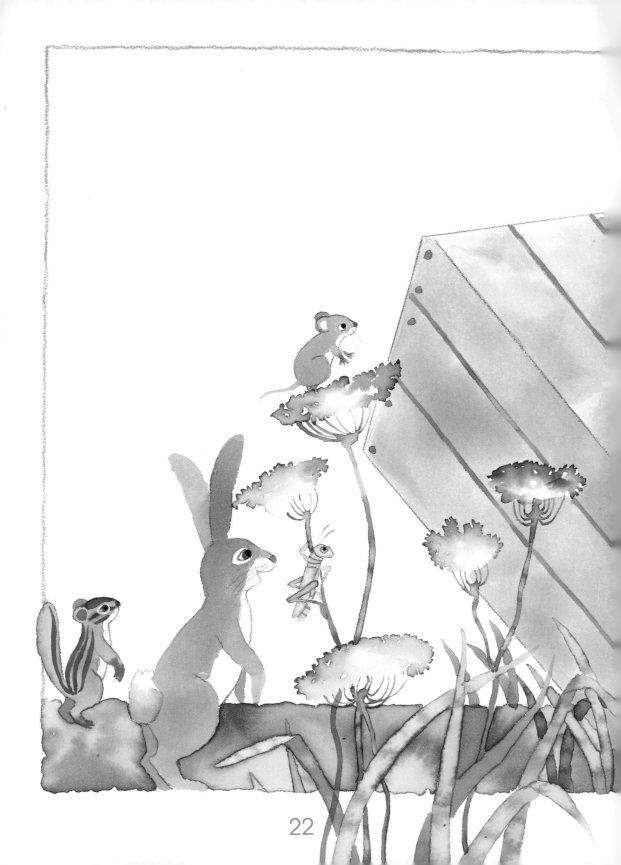

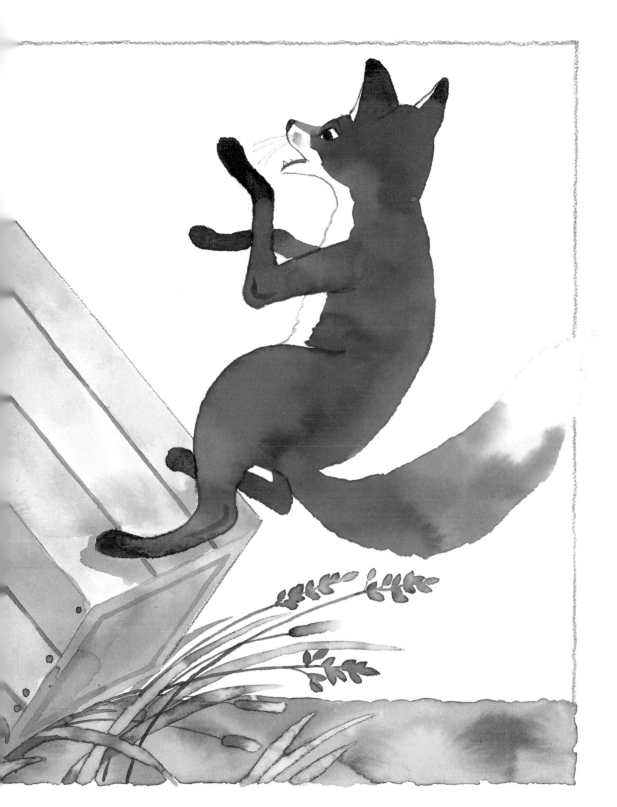

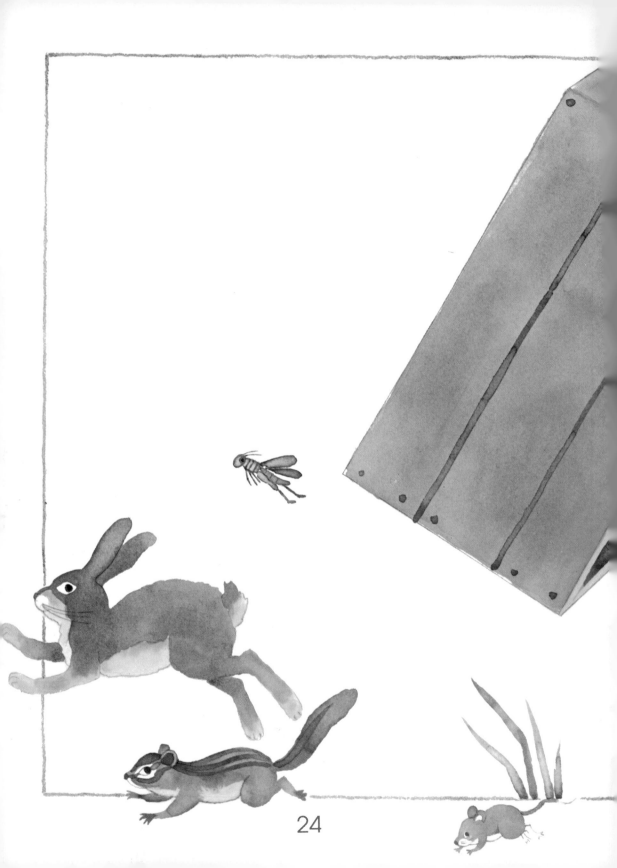

24

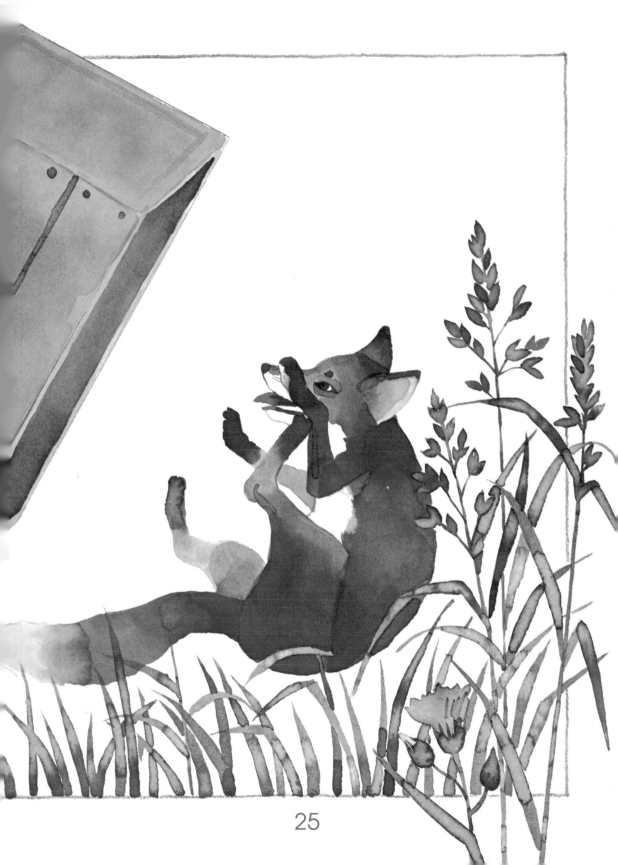

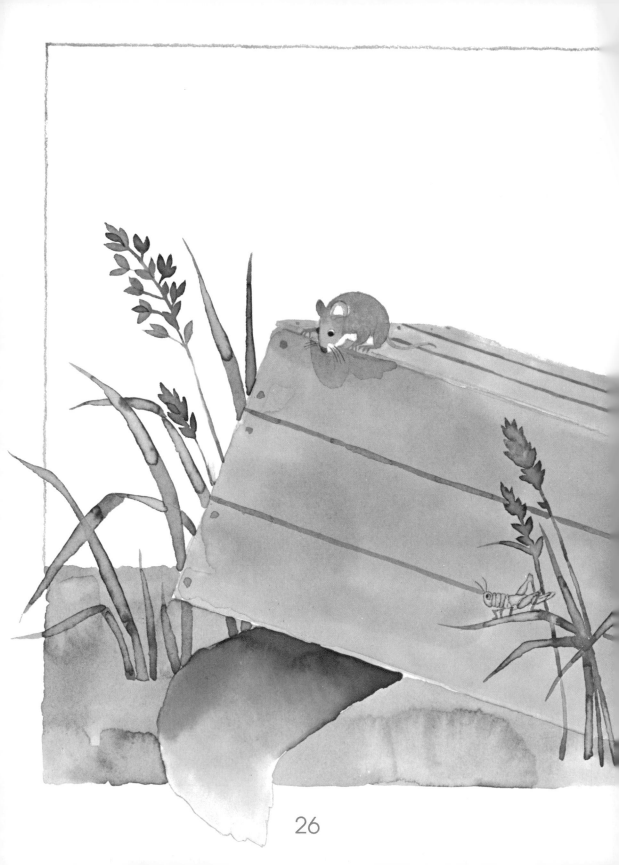

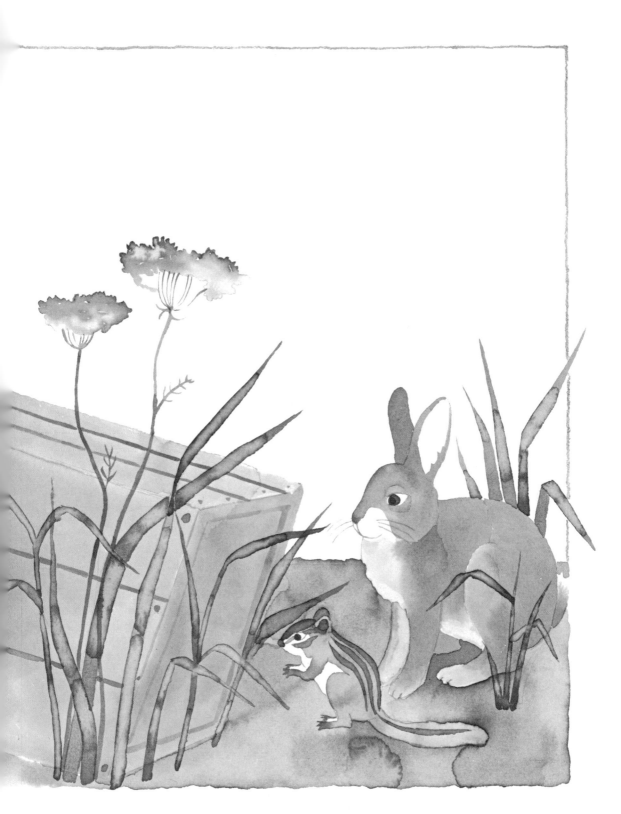

The box sat on the fox.

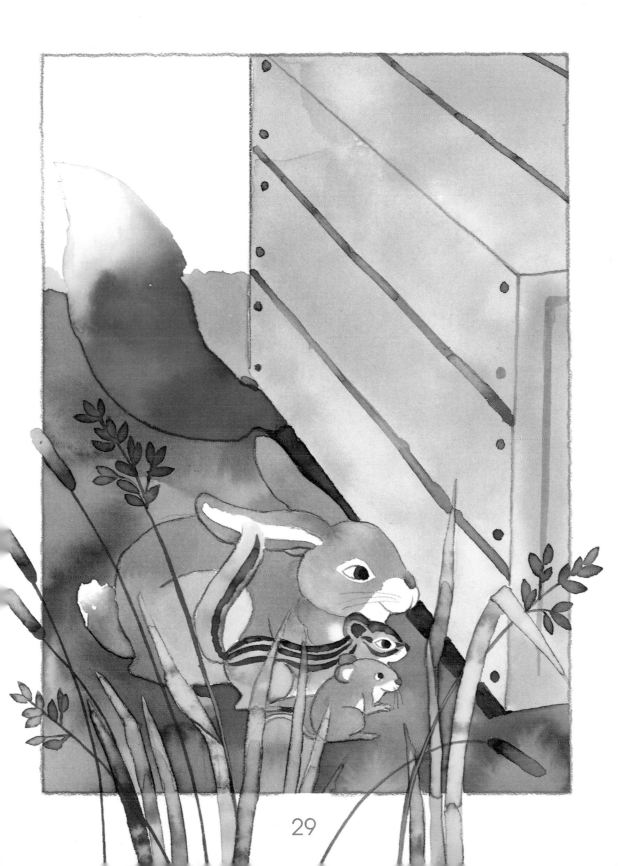

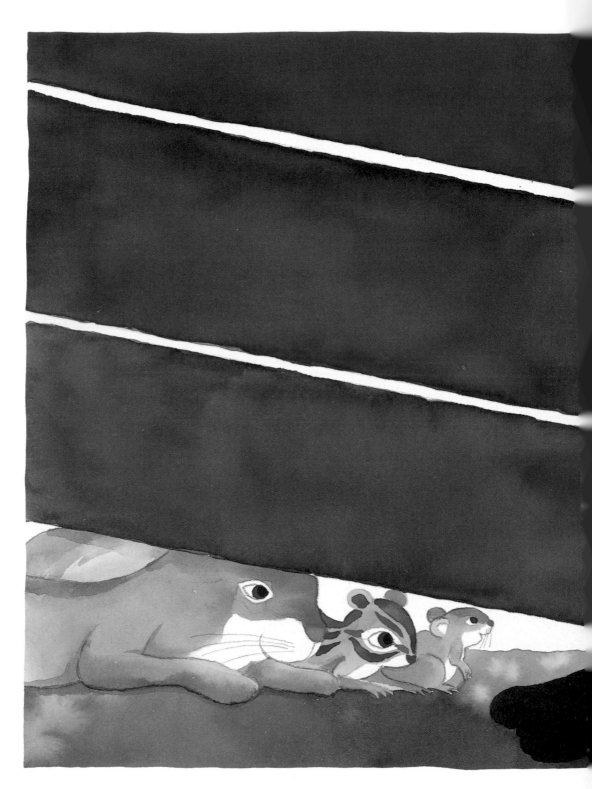

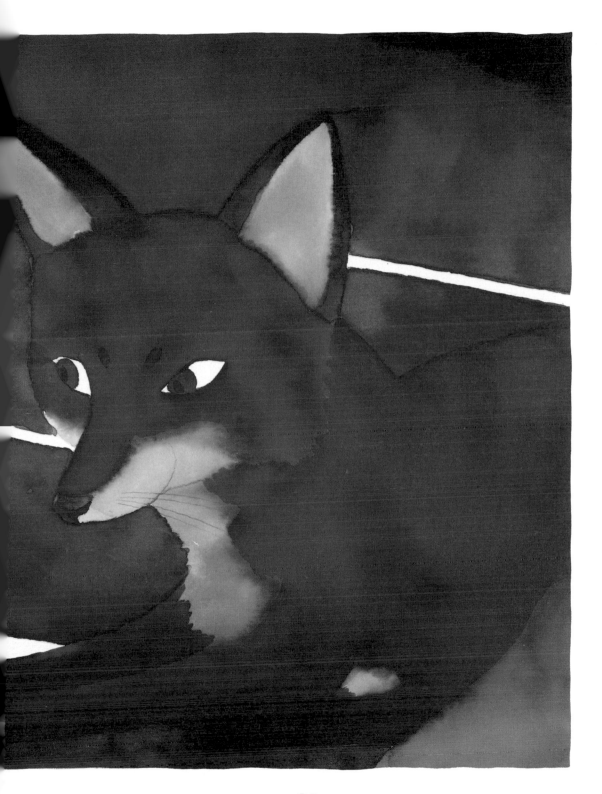

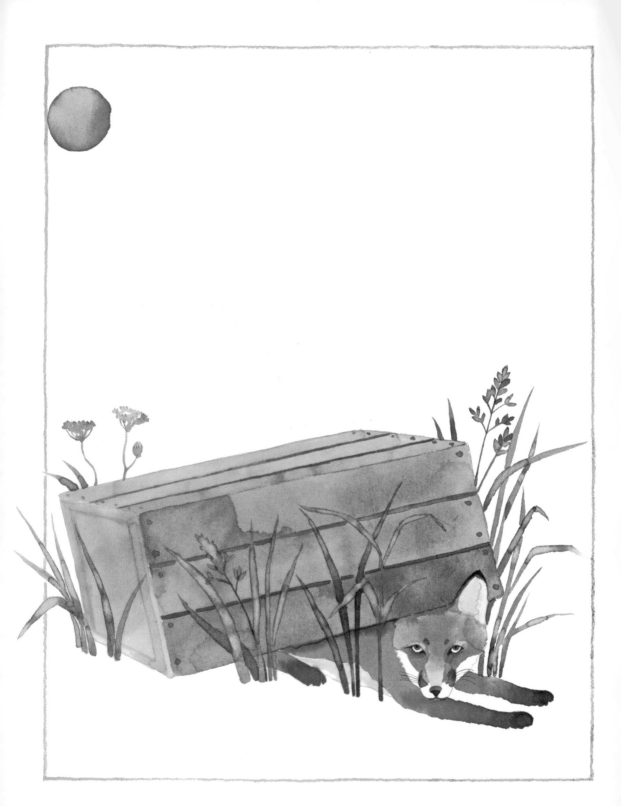